'Harris McCoo & The Rainbow Haggis' is the first in a series of picture books, based on Scottish artist Steven Brown's much-loved 'McCoos'. Developed and written by Shirley Husband, and illustrated by Maurice Hynds of See Saw Creative, they are magical tales of family and friendship, to remind children how beautiful and colourful life can be.

Can you spot Ollie McOwl?

Harris McCoo is a gorgeous old coo
With a twinkle or two in his ee
And he'll tell you a story, in all of its glory
Of how the McCoos came to be.

He looked out to sea, and he whispered to me
"Let me tell you how all of this started
The weather was bad and my mood was so sad
The next day, a wee wish I chanted.

Then I heard a loud squeak and out poked a beak
From the grass popped a mystery creature
He had fur, he had feathers, a hat made of leather
And a mad look across his wee features.

He said, "What's wrong with you, ye miserable coo
Do you not like the weather, you're groaning?
It's Scotland you know, we get rain, sleet and snow
I'll not have you mumping and moaning."

I said, it's so wet, I just wish we could get
Some colour in this pretty place
When the sun comes and shines, on our ocean and pines
There's a big smile on everyone's face.

He sighed, "Aye I see, well just leave that tae me
Do you know what it is that I am?
I'm the Haggis of Ayr, so don't you despair
I'll help you as much as I can."

Can you spot Davy McDug?

"I'll grant you your wish", and he gave a wee swish
Of his hat, as he gave a low bow
"You're a special old coo, and your family too
I'll brighten you up here and now."

Then he kicked up red earth in the place of my birth
Mixed with green grass and plenty blue sky
And the sun shone bright yellow, on this strange wee fellow
We're all rainbow McCoos was my cry!

Now my brothers, my sisters, my wee skin and blisters
My cousins, my family and friends
Are all rainbows of fun, and when all's said and done
Catch the light as it sparkles and bends.

Haggis flashed a last grin, as he blended back in
To the grass and the green countryside
He's as rare as hen's teeth, and he melted beneath
The rich soil with a wave full of pride."

Harris puffed out his chest and up trotted the rest
All the coos in the herd kept the pace
Now the family's all here, and so full of cheer
From the colours that light up their face.

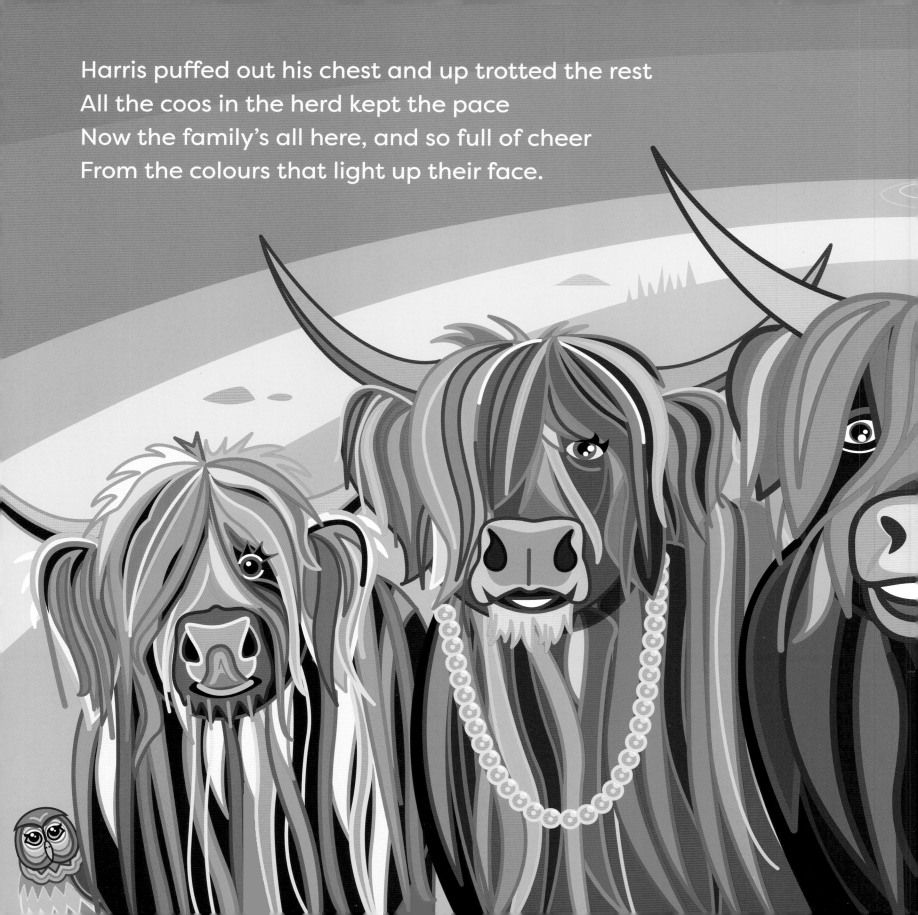

They glint in the light, they're so handsome and bright
Full of life and a sight to behold
So if you're near to Ayr, with a wee while to spare
They'll welcome you into the fold.

And Harris McCoo, that gorgeous old coo
With a twinkle or two in his ee
He'll tell you a story, in all of its glory
Of how the McCoos came to be.

Glossary

Harris McCoo and his amazing family live in Scotland, where we use lots of colourful words. They want everyone to understand their stories, but they love their language too, so we've included just a few Scottish words and expressions for you to enjoy. Just in case you're not quite sure, here's what they mean!

coo – cow
ee – eye
wee – small
ye – you
mumping and moaning – complaining
aye – yes
tae – to
skin and blisters – sisters